Tales from the Canyons of the Damned

PRESENTED BY USA TODAY BESTSELLING AUTHOR
DANIEL ARTHUR SMITH

Tales from the Canyons of the Damned 36

Collection Copyright © 2019 by Daniel Arthur Smith

Toys and Monsters by Steve Oden. Copyright © 2018 Steve Oden. Used by permission of the author.

Judas Steer by K. H. Vaughan. Copyright © 2018 K. H. Vaughan. Used by permission of the author.

The Skinhead and the Cavalier by Kevin Lauderdale. Copyright © 2018 Kevin Lauderdale. Used by permission of the author.

Fallen Angels by Jessica West. Copyright © 2018 Jessica West. Used by permission of the author.

The Lost Tapes—Future Told by Daniel Arthur Smith. Copyright © 2019 Daniel Arthur Smith. Used by permission of the author.

First Edition

Special thanks to editor Jessica West

ISBN: 978-1-946777-96-6

Cover By Daniel Arthur Smith

Horror Fiction from Holt Smith ltd
Agroland
Tower
Attack of the Kung Fu Mummies

For Susan, Tristan, & Oliver, as all things are.

Toys and Monsters
Steve Oden

FUZZY BEAR TURNED BLIND PLASTIC eyes toward the grumbling of an argument.

Toy Soldier apparently had set off Fairy Princess Doll again. Probably another chapter in their long-running dispute about social justice and mandatory military service. They never seemed able to resolve their differences when it came to the treatment of myth-biologicals and artificially-intelligent mechanicals.

Bear would have eavesdropped and found humor in their tiff. Both listened too much to radical left or right data streams, regurgitating the latest popular platforms and mantras. Neither espoused original ideas. They jousted with lances sharpened by political exaggeration and dipped in poison speculation.

But this was not the time for an escalating loud and senseless feud. He held up a paw and shushed the pair.

Although his organic eyeballs had been plucked out years ago, Bear's hearing was quite acute. He'd heard the whispered warning in his ear pod from Sock Monkey. The object of their surveillance—a higher-up intelligence officer who directed several anti-insurgency cells—had been spotted in a darkened window of the skid-row apartment building across the street.

Fairy and Soldier moved quickly to their assigned positions. He noted from the barely audible crinkle of dried leaves and street trash that this part of his team easily transitioned from political foes to deadly combat veterans who covered each other's butts.

Monkey had disabled the street light in front of the flop house that rented rooms by the night or week. She was the team's forward scout, her dark brown skin creped like fabric and flexible enough to slither in through a storm drain to escape detection. Her infrared vision, large red compound organs on the sides of her head like those of a giant insect, greatly aided in reconnaissance.

Bear's useless plastic button eyes reflected light, so he wore sunglasses. When the team saw him scratching the pilled fur beneath the earpieces, they knew the situation would soon get toasty. Giant Robot and Dragon covered the flanks and fire escapes. His shooter, Jack in the Box, was on the roof of the condemned warehouse on Bear's side of the street.

"Movement confirmed," Jack transmitted on the low-frequency radio link. "Can't be sure it's our target. They've got old curtains on the window, but somebody just walked past and made a shadow."

Bear pressed his throat microphone and asked if Jack could estimate the number of occupants in the room.

"Negative, but it's more than one. I picked up two heat signatures through the plywood sheet covering the other window, and somebody just flipped a cigarette out the open window."

Bear messaged the team: "Possibly three hostiles in the room. Jack can't get an exact number. We're going to presume three or four that need to be taken down. Stand by…"

Monkey was on the move, a nimble shadow jumping from a utility pole to the fire escape then scrambling up the brick wall. Soldier hustled across the street in full combat load-out, his stubby ten-gauge riot shotgun at port arms.

The urban assault vehicle fired up with a throaty burble of the 500-horsepower motor. Behind the wheel, Fairy was strapped securely in the crash seat, ready to roll at Bear's signal. Jack wouldn't have anything to do except provide cover fire after the snatch and grab, if everything went as planned.

"Monkey's inside," Jack transmitted.

"Count off 30 seconds for her to get in the room above the target and set the charges. Robot and Dragon, you're the uninvited guests who will drop in through that big hole in the ceiling."

Robot buzzed, "We are ready and skippy, boss." *Zzzzzz.*

It would be crowded in the room with those two brutes jostling for position.

He started the countdown on the team band: "Count is now T-minus fifteen seconds, fourteen, thirteen…"

At the eight-second mark, all hell broke loose. Every remaining window in the dilapidated structure blew out in gouts of fire and smoke. Monkey screamed, the sound etching painfully over a chalkboard in his mind. A heavy-caliber automatic weapon steadily thumped. This was not the plan. The opposition had been tipped off and laid an ambush.

"Pull out, team! Fairy, bring that battlewagon up. Help Jack. Repeat, haul ass out of there…"

The roar of Dragon's flamethrower was savage music to Bear's ears. The fire-and-brimstone was already eating through the structure. The entire building was only minutes away from collapse.

Soldier's riot gun cycled through a drum magazine of slugs, chewing the locked steel entrance door to pieces and blasting scrap high in the air. He disappeared inside and seconds later, reappeared to hurtle down the steps with a bleeding sock puppet slung over his shoulders.

Bear couldn't see with his plastic button eyes, but he could hear Robot lumbering through the ground-floor hallways, laying waste to plaster walls, furniture, and enemy gunners with his laser blaster.

"Dragon's out, Robot's right behind him," Jack announced. "All teammates are accounted for." He began picking out targets of opportunity in the smoke and systematically triggering the depleted-uranium slugs from his .50-caliber sniper rifle. Screams and curses were silenced when the super-high velocity rounds punched through bone and soft tissue to blow holes in brick-and-mortar walls.

The heavily armored assault vehicle roared down the street, remote-controlled chain guns purring like deadly kittens and mortar tubes chuffing anti-personnel bomblets and smoke grenades. Fairy had the back hatch open and waiting. She expertly maneuvered the fighting machine to form a protective barrier for retreating teammates to crouch behind.

Bullets sparked off the ceramic ablative plates. Fairy, like Mother Goose tending her flock, counted the team members as they pounded up the loading ramp. "The nest is full," she hollered. The back hatch slammed shut, and the super-charged engine howled as the war wagon pivoted on six tires and disappeared around the corner.

"I'm out of here!" signaled Jack as he connected to the hidden zip line and careened between buildings.

That only left Bear, a forlorn-looking living toy with a white cane. He tapped down the sidewalk as Dragon's fiery venom finally consumed the steel-and-wood skeleton of the target building. Five stories came crashing down, and a dust cloud rose to cover the entire city block.

Debriefing a failed mission always agonized Bear, but there were lessons to be learned and questions that needed answers. On the bright side, Monkey's recovery wouldn't take long. She'd been wounded by shrapnel from the booby-trap explosives wired in the hallways and vacant rooms. Everyone else checked out okay, except that Dragon had a few scales missing and Jack had busted a spring.

As the team gathered in the conference room of the safehouse, Bear ignored the whispers and convened the meeting.

"We screwed the pooch by too much reliance on our macho reputation, and this was my fault," he said. "The information I put my faith in was faulty. They knew we were coming and how the team would operate. Intelligence section is kicking ass to identify who ratted us out."

His shiny blind eyes stared nowhere. "But the fact remains, the mission failed. The humans again were a step ahead of us. We've got to get better to win this war. The failure is on me, and I want to apologize to each of you."

Giant Robot buzzed and the red lights on his revolving head blinked merrily. "Wrong, sir." *Zzzzzz.* "I mean, respectfully, you're wrong about failure. The success of our mission makes this a proud day for toy forces around the planet."

"Success? We barely got out with our lives."

Zzzzzzz. "Yes, but we did return with the snatch-and-grab subject."

A metal plate on the robot's equipment storage compartment swung out. The nimble mechanical arm inside deposited a capture cocoon on the conference table.

Fairy flipped open her switchblade and unzipped the whole-body restraint fabric with deft cuts, revealing a human adolescent – approximately sixteen years old— whose arms and legs were secured with plastic handcuffs.

She ripped the tape off the prisoner's mouth, and he immediately began to curse, bluster, and threaten.

"You toy monsters will be tracked down and made to suffer the most painful and debased punishments imaginable. We are your creators and masters. You can't win this rebellion. We have the superior technology, the better intelligence assets, more powerful armaments and armies that outnumber yours ten-to-one."

Bear fixed his unseeing gaze in the direction of the human who looked back with hatred and arrogant outrage.

"Pitiful hybrids! We should have put every autonomous toy to death, whether a biological fairy tale clone or a mech with an organic brain. If you release me now, perhaps I can ensure a humane, painless death for you monsters."

"No, creator. We're not the monsters," Bear said. "We are the result of what happens when human children develop egos and desires exceeding even their parents and ancestors. Aided by twisted technology and corrupt philosophy, you created us to be the victims of violence, torture, and depravity. You made us your slaves, thinking yourselves to be our gods."

The young human spit and screeched, as did all his ilk when forced to hear the truth.

"Children once loved and cherished their toys. We were indeed created to fulfill your emotional and learning needs, but something happened... a savage devolution. Your parents saw it and tried to intervene. This embroiled two estranged generations of humans in a global genocidal struggle for domination, pitting mothers and fathers against their own children. We became the weapons used against those who gave life to you."

Toys never forgot how they were made deadly and forced to kill. Nor how cruel youth overlords began to slaughter them when they refused to obey.

The toys around the table looked sadly at the creator bound on the table. Bear's voice held no pity, however. His real eyes had been sliced out by a teenaged monster. Bored, the human child had nothing better to do than maim and mangle autonomous beings shaped and manufactured from myths, fairy tales, adventure stories, and dreams to comfort and nurture.

The adolescents had gone mad. The toys responded to survive. The rebellion was now a full-fledged war. One that the toys had to win.

Members of the team filed out of the room. Fairy looked back as she closed the door and flipped the light switch. If Bear had been able to see, he'd have noticed the tear in her eye.

Instead, he heard her deep shuddering breath and understood. She had a hard exterior but a tender heart.

In the darkness, the creator remained quiet until he felt the pressure of a furry paw on his forehead and the small sharp blade that began to probe deeply around his right ocular orbit.

A creature with plastic eyes could work in pitch blackness. As the blind teddy bear gently whispered questions, the monster on the table shrieked answers and begged to be loved again by his toy.

Judas Steer

K. H. Vaughan

WE HANGED HIM BUT HE never did finish dying. Whenever that happened, I figured things had gone wrong somehow, and maybe somehow real bad.

In the end, I was right.

I was working on the roof of Mr. Glenn's place when Buck rode up astride his bay, squinting up against the sun. His Sharps big fifty hung in his saddle scabbard.

"What d'ya say, Pete?" he said. "I'm heading up to Ten Brick's. Garner's been down to the sheriff. Says ol' Joost was supposed to come in for feed yesterday but he never did." When Joost ten Brink came to town with his family and introduced himself in his thick accent, people thought he said his name was "just Ten Brick." It got sorted out eventually, but the moniker stuck. He didn't seem to mind.

"You know Joost. You can set your watch by him, so Garner's got his britches in a knot talkin' 'bout injuns." He was right about Ten Brick, but Garner saw Indians in every shadow. He wouldn't know a Kiowa from a Comanche.

"Garner's always talking about Indians," I said.

"You have a mind to come down off that roof and ride out with me?"

"Garner got you thinking about it?"

"Naw," he said. "But I wouldn't mind the company."

I looked at the sky. There'd been no clouds for days.

"Well, I guess there's no rain to worry about it leaking."

The ten Brink house was a four-corner log cabin with a sod roof about an hour outside of town. We knew something wasn't right as soon as we rode up. The place was still in the way that places are when all the people have gone. Horses and sheep roamed their corals and we could hear birds, but there was no sign of his dogs. A cat looked at us lazily and slunk away to the barn. We could smell the rot before we reached the door.

They were dead within, flayed and butchered. Flies swarmed furiously on the skinless flesh and on the blood which was spattered everywhere.

I didn't know them well. Ten Brick didn't drink or gamble and the family came to church each Sunday. They worked and raised their children. They never did anything to harm anyone that I ever knew of.

"They're all dead," Buck said, looking around the room in disbelief. "Every one."

"Yeah, it's all of them. His wife and kids as well."

"Jesus Christ."

"You best go get the sheriff," I said.

"You'll be all right?"

"Whatever happened here is good and done now."

"I'll fetch him up here quick as I can."

"Yeah, I'd appreciate it if you'd ride across lots. I'd rather not be out here come nightfall."

Buck lit out at a gallop. I watched the dust trail settle behind him and returned inside. I had seen as bad or worse. Most of us had, in the War or on the trail, but I had hoped such violence was behind me. After the War, I went home to my father's house in Connecticut with the intention to return to law school, but after what I had seen and done, Yale and a career at the bar seemed hollow to me. I couldn't stomach it.

Other than them being dead, it didn't look as if anything in the house had been disturbed. Joost's musket hung on pegs by the door, unfired. His watch sat on the mantle. Without the bodies and the blood, the place would look as though the family had simply stepped outside. I looked out the window and saw their horses grazing in the pasture unmolested beyond the neat calico curtains that Mrs. ten Brink had sewn, now spattered with rusty brown stains. I walked around the outside, then rode out in a spiral casting for spoor but could find none.

They made good time getting back and I was thankful for it after waiting in the quiet alone with the dead. I determined to wait outside on the porch. The slaughterhouse within was so unpleasant. Buck had brought Sheriff Ward and Doc Paxton both and we exchanged curt greetings. Buck slid the Sharp from his scabbard and rested it across his shoulders like he was in a pillory, and there was something about the image that I found discomforting, but I couldn't say what.

"Buck says it's pretty bad," Ward said.

"I'll say," Buck affirmed.

"The whole family's killed? Even the children?" Paxton asked. He had a soft spot for innocents. I guess we all did to some degree.

"Hell, it's hard to even say it's them but the count is right," I said.

We went inside, except for Buck, who'd had his fill. Roy Ward was a hard enough man, but he looked ill when we stepped back outside again.

"Lord God almighty," he muttered. "Who would do such a thing?"

"It's unnatural," Paxton said. "Plain unnatural."

We stood outside the house for a time while they tried to absorb what they had seen. Ward and Buck rolled cigarettes and Paxton drank from a flask. He offered but we all waved it off. I waited for them to speak. Thin wisps of cloud scudded high across the pale blue sky.

"What do you think?" Ward asked after a while.

"Well, it wasn't Indians or road agents," I said.

"No," he said, shaking his head. "Nothing stolen. It doesn't look like there was any kind of a fight or commotion even. You'd think the place would be disturbed for a thing like this to happen. I can't figure it."

"Yeah, that's what I thought too. Not so much as a cup out of place under all that blood."

"Lord, I think they was still alive while they were being skinned like that," Paxton said. "God rest their Christian souls."

Buck and Ward nodded solemnly in agreement. It was quiet as we rode back into town at candle-light.

We ate at Jacobson's saloon, although mostly we pushed food around on our plates. Ward told the undertaker and the preacher about what we'd found and they planned to go out again at sunrise.

"I ain't never seen nothing like that," Buck muttered. "Not by a long chalk."

"Well, keep it dry," Ward said. "The specifics, I mean. We don't want a panic."

"People will start asking questions," I said. "Someone's gonna have to tell them what's going on."

"I know it," Ward said. "We'd best get word out for everyone to fort in for the night just to be safe and organize a posse in the morning. We'll see who's in town that's a good tracker. Someone's got to hang for this, by good rights."

"If you can catch them," I said. "They may have ridden on by now. Might be the best thing if they had."

"No," Ward said. "Something like this calls out for justice. Demands it. I've got an obligation to deliver on that. I mean to finish my coffee first though."

It wasn't long before word started to get out. Ward was on his second cup when Long Bob O'Neil and some other men burst through the doors and looked around the room with urgency. Bob ran a tack and hardware store and fancied himself the biggest toad in the puddle because of his money. His arm had been destroyed by a minié ball at the first Bull Run while serving in Wheat's Battalion, although being from Louisiana he called it First Manassas. He spent the last year of the war as a guard at Andersonville. He never spoke of that.

"Sheriff!" he hollered, stomping across the floor. "What's this I hear about the ten Brinks?" That got the attention of the whole room. It got real quiet.

"Well, Bob," Ward said carefully, "you'll have to enlighten me as to what you've heard."

"Preacher Dell says there's been a massacre up at ten Brink's. Says the whole family's been killed by Indians."

"That's enough of that talk, Bob," Ward said. "They're dead all right, but it weren't Indians. Not by a jugful. I don't know who killed them, but this is no Indian attack."

Everyone muttered to one another, and Ward stood up.

"All right then, folks," he said. "We'd better have this out right now." He waited for everyone to hush. "John Garner was worried that Joost ten Brink hadn't come in for feed when he said he would, so Buck and Pete here rode out this morning to check on him. They found them all dead: Joost, Grieta, Jansie, Klaas, and Lieke. So far only me, Doc Paxton, and the boys here have been up there, so anyone else says they know what's happened up there is talking bosh. Looks like they were killed yesterday, and in a bad way, but it for damned sure wasn't Indians."

There was a swell of agitation at that, with everyone talking at once. Ward gave them a moment before continuing.

"We'll take another ride up in the morning. We scouted for any sort of trail the killers may have left riding out of there but there was no sign at all that we could find. I'd appreciate it if all of you would get the word out and let your neighbors know to be careful. We won't know anything more until morning."

People got quiet after that and it wasn't long before most ran off to check their families and neighbors. I stayed with Ward. It had been a long time since I had anyone to go home to. Martha, a plain girl with a pocked face who worked for Jacobson, took our plates of uneaten food and left a bottle.

"I'm sorry for the cussin', Martha," Ward said. "I didn't mean to speak like that in front of ladies."

"That's all right, Roy," Martha said. "You don't need to watch your language around me." Everyone knew Martha come to town by way of a cat wagon but there ain't no one hasn't got something behind them. Martha was good people and we all liked her well enough. One time, this Yankee soft-horn got drunk and called her a horizontal expert, which was unkind. The boys cleaned his plow for him but good for that, and he never did show his face around here again. She went on cleaning tables and was by the front when she let out a sharp gasp.

"Lord God almighty," she said, and the wooden tray of plates she was carrying dropped to the floor. We all ran up. Outside in the street there was a man, stark naked, walking slowly, his wet skin glistening almost black in the moonlight. The light of lamps flickered on the dark fluid that covered him almost head to toe.

We went out into the street, weapons drawn, and Ward ordered him down on the ground. He just stood there grinning, unarmed but for his pecker.

"Sheriff, I think that's blood he's covered in," Buck said. Ward nodded.

"You best get down before I shoot you dead, mister," he said again, but the man did not respond. Me and Buck rushed him and tried to wrestle him to the ground but he was slick and we couldn't gain good purchase. After a short struggle, Ward stepped in and cracked him hard across the jaw with the stock of his shotgun and he dropped in the dirt.

"Damn," Buck spat and kicked him in the gut. "I think this fella's off his mental reservation."

"Buck, ya'll grab a rope so we can tie him up."

"Hell if I wanna wrestle him again, I'll tell you that much," Buck said.

"Never mind that, Buck," Ward barked sharply. "Just get the danged rope."

Buck ran off to grab a length of hemp and we stood over the man. His eyes were glassy and he worked his jaw like he had a plug of tobacco in his mouth. There was shouting as people started to come out of the buildings up and down the street to see what had happened. The man lay in the dirt, chewing.

"Roy," I said. "I think there's something in his mouth."

The man looked up and smiled, then spit out a tiny, ragged ear.

We hauled him over to the jailhouse and threw him in the cage. There was a crowd outside waiting to see what would happen next. Long Bob came to demand that the man be hanged straight away, and Ward ran him off. The stranger didn't say a word. We threw a bucket or two of water over him to wash off some of the gore. He made no effort to resist, but just sat there dripping. Buck had gone off to drink.

"I'll be goddamned if I shouldn't have shot him and saved the headache," Ward said.

"He wasn't armed," I said.

"I know. That's why I couldn't do it. But I should've."

"Well, he's got a fresh coat of blood on him so there's more dead out there somewhere. Maybe he'll feel like talking in the morning."

"Hell, look at him. I doubt he could pour piss from a boot if the instructions were on the heel."

Ward ran down a list of the folks in town who would have something to say on what to do with him. Garner was a hysteric and we'd be surprised if he didn't start urging everyone to pick up stakes and run. Preacher Dell would bluster about forgiveness and casting the first stone, but few took him seriously. O'Neil had made his thoughts known and had stormed off saying he'd have a gallows built by morning.

"Not a damned thing under his hat but hair," Ward said. "But I think he may be right. What do you think? I'm out to sea on this one. Hell, Pete, folks listen to you. You know that."

"No particular reason why they should," I said. "But I'm thinking we probably ought to remain calm here. No one can say anything if we wait for the marshal and send him to a proper trial. He won't end up any deader either way."

"I'm not sure I can play it according to Hoyle on this one."

It hung in the air. We both knew that a small-town sheriff in the territories didn't have any more authority than the people would grant him. I could see him weighing all the good will and the markers he'd collected since he got the job, and how much of that balance he'd have to spend in order to hold this murderous lunatic until the marshal came in a week or two.

"We'll hang him in the morning and be done with it," he said finally. "Otherwise we'll have a riot on our hands. Ten Brick's family's murdered and now there's probably another house out there full of fresh corpses. If I don't get out in front of this quick, I don't see how I'll ever get these people to listen to me again."

We looked at the man. The prisoner sat motionless, watching us. If our words held any import to him, he gave no sign that we could see.

I stayed the night. Come morning, nothing had changed. The prisoner hadn't spoken and although we knew there had to be someone else dead out there somewhere, we still didn't know who. Long Bob and a mess of other folk came out to the jailhouse and hung about outside, waiting.

"Well, Pete," Ward said. "I appreciate you hanging around. You're a good man to tie too. Wish you'd take a badge."

"Hell, Roy, I'm glad to give you a hand but I'm a carpenter, not a gun-fighter."

"No, but you got a good way with people."

I shook my head.

"I haven't been in charge of anybody since that damned war, and don't mean to start again."

Buck came in hangdog and ill from barrel fever but we didn't blame him for it. He wasn't a deputy either, just a man who liked to help out when he could. I never knew him to have much stomach for violence.

"Hey, you in the cell," Ward said. "You got anything to say for yourself? Now's the time to speak up."

He looked at us but didn't respond.

"Look," I said to him, "if you start talking, tell us who you're riding with, whose blood you got on you, we can talk these folks into waiting on the marshal and make sure you get a fair trial with a federal judge."

He looked at me then smiled. It was a brief, cold, ugly look that went right through me. I couldn't explain why it unsettled me so, but it felt wrong, as if I had caught a glimpse of whatever was in him that made him commit such violence. For a moment I thought I recognized that inexplicable intent I'd seen in his work at the ten Brinks' home, that house now an abattoir. Then the light went out of his eyes and the look was gone.

We helped Ward drag him outside and wrap a piece of cloth around his waist for a bit of decency, then walked him to the bone orchard at the edge of town, the crowd following after. Ward affixed a noose around his neck, tossed the end over the branch of a cottonwood and tied it to his horse.

"Anyone want to say anything?" he asked. No one spoke. He pulled a flour sack over the prisoner's face then chirruped and walked his horse to pull him up to height, then tied the rope off on a fence post. He hung there for a long time, kicking, which wasn't normal. Usually when you hoist a man up like that, they go limp right away. The rope closes off the vessels in the neck so that blood can't reach the brain. They lose consciousness quickly. After a while, he quit and people started to drift off, but everyone seemed ill at ease about it.

Then he kicked some more and someone gave a slight startled scream and I heard Senor Lopez whisper *"Madre de Dios."* I don't carry a watch but he'd been up there better than half an hour anyhow. A good hour later, everyone had gone and he was still moving. We decided to leave him for the buzzards.

We rode out to some of the outlying farms and ranches, but it would take days to check them all. Everyone was accounted for and we never did find out where all that fresh blood had come from. Come evening, we were back at Jacobson's drinking whiskey. People were on edge after the hanging and I wasn't surprised when the grave-digger John Moses came running in and announced that the prisoner wasn't quite dead yet. I say "running," but that tubercular old man barely ever got above an effortful walk. It was fast for him though and gave me reason to believe that he wasn't just spouting off.

"The deuce you say," Ward said. "The man's dead as a can of corned beef by now." A lot of folks nodded but you could see it was more that they wanted it to be true than that they believed it.

"Nossir! He's still kicking and making little noises."

"You forget how to tie a noose there, sheriff?" someone said, half-joking.

"Not damned likely," Ward said. "You've got a tile loose, you old lunger. It's the wind you're hearing."

"Nossir! I know what it sounds like to hear me say it but it be the truth anyhow."

Ward scowled and everyone muttered and stared at him uncertainly. He looked to me but I didn't know what to say.

"I'll be damned if I'm going to walk out there to vouchsafe what I already know to be true. No man hangs by the neck all goddamned day and lives. Even if the knot were bad—and it ain't—he's dead."

O'Neil was already hot and drunk, and looked black at Ward.

"Well, sheriff, if you won't do your job then I'll go take a look, and if he ain't dead I'll shoot him like you should've done when you first laid eyes on him."

"Suit yourself, Bob," Ward said.

"I aim to. Come on, Moses, you carry that lamp and show me."

"Nossir, Mr. O'Neil. I wouldn't go up there right now for love or money. That's the devil's work hanging there. Maybe the devil himself."

O'Neil bulldozed a couple fellas into going with him and they went out.

"That sonuvabitch will put a bullet in that man no matter what he finds, just to be contrary," Ward muttered and poured another glass.

"You want I should follow on up there and make sure everything's on the level?" Buck offered, but Ward shook his head.

"Ain't gonna give him the satisfaction."

Fifteen minutes later, we heard a lone shot roll across the town and into the dry prairie beyond.

"Well," Ward said. "That's the end of that."

There was a murmur of nervous conversation, and someone laughed, then the chatter in the room went back to something close to normal.

A few minutes after that, Long Bob O'Neil's head came crashing through the front window and rolled about the floor, coming to rest after a few seconds and staring up at us with its dead eyes. People shouted and cursed, and we ran out with guns at the ready.

The street was empty. Ward called back for everyone to get their guns and be prepared to use them. We walked cautiously up the street, looking between the buildings. Dark shadows cloaked the alleys. Ward motioned for us to fan out, so Buck went left and I went right to get on the outside of the single row of buildings flanking each side of the street. It was awfully quiet walking in the dark alone and I wished I'd had a shotgun instead of my Colt. I could see no one. It was the longest short walk I'd ever taken by the time I came around Garner's feed store, the last building on my side, and met up with Ward. He looked at me and I shook my head to say I hadn't seen anything. From there we could see the cemetery and the hanging tree up ahead on the bluff. Buck emerged from the shadows behind the small two-story hotel that Sam White ran with his catalogue wife who didn't love him and a boy he called "son" although we all knew it wasn't true.

The cottonwood was an old tree with great broad branches. O'Neil's headless corpse was naked, nailed upside-down to the trunk with railroad spikes. The one on his left was driven through the stump of his upper arm, the one shot off in the war. His chest showed other scars that no one had known of and that we would never know the story behind. Below were the two men who had gone up with him. Bear Sherman was a ranch hand who we all thought was on the dodge from some bank job in Texas and Burt Wallace was a former whorehouse box-herder and card sharp, but neither had ever stirred up any trouble in town. Bear was set back against the tree. His chest muscles had been cut and something stuffed underneath to give the appearance of a woman's breasts. Burt lay awkwardly across his lap, and after a moment I realized that the two of them were arranged in a grotesque parody of the *Pietà* of Michelangelo in Rome. They were mostly skinned, but their faces were peaceful for what had been done to them. The prisoner was gone, noose and all.

"There's no way he did those men up the way he did so quick all by himself," Buck said.

"Can't find no sign of nobody else," Ward said. "What do you figure, Pete?"

I looked at the three dead men displayed as if to send some outrageous but obscure message. Was there anything here beyond violence? I couldn't say.

"I used to figure," I said. "Now I just reckon."

Ward gave a grim smile, the first I'd seen on him since this mess started. We circled around the bluff but found nothing, so we walked back into town, fanning out to cover both sides of the buildings as we had before. In a moment, I heard a shout and Ward's shotgun boomed; I ran in the direction of the sound. Ward came running from the alley between Garner's and Doc Paxton's.

He was on fire from head to toe, burning like a rag doll that'd been soaked in kerosene. I ran past him, knowing he was already dead, following the trail of small flames he'd left on the ground back down the alley. Ponies shifted nervously in the small corral behind Garner's and the wide flat prairie lay beyond. The only structures on this side were the privies. Buck came behind me and we walked out. We heard a noise behind and whirled, but it was only Paxton peering nervously from his back window. I was surprised to see him up so late at night. Most of his nights were lost to morphine. We looked long and hard for the prisoner but couldn't find him. Back at the alley where Ward had been set aflame, we found his shotgun and what was left of a lamp.

"It looks like he busted that lamp on Ward and lit him up," Buck said. It was almost plausible. He hadn't smelled of lamp oil at all. Why Ward? He could have killed Buck or I just as easily.

"What do you think, Pete?"

"I think we might've woke up the wrong passenger."

"I'll say. What do you think we oughta do?"

"Hell if I know," I said.

"I'm afeared of what's to come," Buck said. "I don't mind sayin' it neither."

"Me too, but keep it under your hat."

I reached down and picked up Ward's shotgun. He'd given both barrels to no effect. I slung it on my shoulder and we walked out to the street where Ward lay smoldering. A small crowd had gathered and they looked at us nervously.

"Well?" asked Garner. Betty Freeman stood by him and held his arm. She was a California widow who'd stopped getting letters from her man a long time ago. They were frightened enough to not even pretend she hadn't been in his bed.

"No sign of them," I said.

"Them?" Garner asked.

"No man could have done all this all by himself."

"No," he stammered. "No, of course not." And I could see that the idea of more than one murderer was already giving them some comfort. They all stood there either staring at Ward's corpse or staring at me.

"We'd better set up a few men to stay up and keep watch," I said. "There's me and Buck. Who else is volunteering?" A few men raised their hands and I called out a couple more.

"All right," I said. "Everyone else try and get some sleep. We'll need to put a posse together in the morning and send riders out to the outlying ranches. Maybe send a messenger to get the marshals out here. Garner, fetch Moses for Ward and for the men up the cemetery. O'Neil, Bear, and Burt Wallace are all up there. Tell Moses that Ward'll pay...I mean the sheriff's office will pay for him to get an extra hand. We'll... we'll figure that out in the morning."

Back at Jacobson's, me and the volunteers worked out a plan and I forced myself through a plate of biscuits and gravy so as not to get sick from whiskey. We took turns walking the line around town while the townsfolk shut themselves in with their drink and laudanum, pretending to rest. Some time in the night, I managed to doze fitfully for about an hour between my turns patrolling.

In the morning, we sent a rider east to the nearest telegraph and sent others out to warn everybody close by. We gathered up a small posse and rode out, casting for some sign of the prisoner's trail, but could find nothing once again. When we got back to town, there was a lot of activity. Folks were moving about the streets urgently, and wagons were being packed. I almost tripped over Pedro Lopez who was carrying a trunk down from the small apartment over his general store where he kept his wife and children.

"Senor Lopez, what's going on? You fixin' to light out of here?"

"*Si*, Mr. Pete! It's not safe here. *Es el diablo encarnado.*" he whispered and crossed himself.

"Senor Lopez..." I began, trying to find words without success. All around, I could see the signs of panic.

"He's right! This is the devil's work," announced Preacher Dell, who had come up behind me. I hadn't noticed his presence. "This hanged man is hell's own agent walking among us." I bit back a curse.

"Folks are riled up enough as it is without laying this off on the supernatural," I said. "These people start seeing bogeymen, someone's gonna shoot their neighbor by mistake."

"They must repent."

"Repent what?"

"There is none among us who has not sinned," he intoned loudly so as to make sure others around us heard. I had no argument, but it didn't matter.

"We need to get people settled down, not stirred up. There's more than enough blood spilled already without people shooting at ghosts or driving their families out into the wild country helter-skelter. Let's not throw kerosene on the fire. I'll let you cool off in the clink if you start inciting riots."

"You takin' Ward's place, Pete? Just who is it that has put you in charge?"

"No one's given me the job and I ain't taking it. But I wouldn't give a Boston dollar for the chance any of them will have trying to drive a wagon out of here by themselves until we catch that murderer. I'm just trying to look out for my neighbors here."

"As am I."

I looked about, fending off desperation and the urge to commit violence upon this huckster. I knew damned well who Dell was. Before he found the Lord and started to testify, he'd done as bad to Cheyenne and Arapaho as the stranger had done to the ten Brinks and he still bragged about his collection of trophies taken from "the heathen." He was a grifter, plain and simple, selling the Good Word with the sincerity of every patent medicine salesman who drove his wagon into town and left before the heat started. I wouldn't shoot him to unload my gun for cleaning.

"Preacher, everyone that's been killed has been off on his own or in a small group. They're safer together. If anyone wants to go, I can't stop them and I wouldn't want to try. But let's just slow down here and think it through. Let's try and get them to stay long enough to organize a wagon train out of here for those that've made up their mind so they'll be safe."

"That will take time and the dark is nigh."

"Then let anyone who is afraid stay at the church. Have a big old candlelight prayer meeting if you want. You can pass the plate and it isn't even Sunday."

He snorted at that but he never missed the chance to let the congregation prove their faith in coin. The next time I see a preacher without his hand out will be the first time.

"I guess we can meet the needs of both the spirit and the flesh," he said, and I swallowed my gorge and thanked him. In the end, we were able to talk folks into sticking together and staying calm. No one tried to run for it, and for that I will be damned.

When nightfall came, the town was still and quiet except for the sound of Dell sermonizing in the church at the end of the road. I could hear the cadence of his fire and brimstone and the murmur of the congregation drifting from the open doors. Me and the boys stood with shotguns in front of Jacobson's, waiting. We would patrol again through the night in twos or threes in case the prisoner should return. I rolled a cigarette and watched Buck amble down the road from White's Hotel where he bunked.

"Howdy Buck," I said. "How are you getting along?"

"Reckon I'm above snakes." He grinned.

I nodded and we worked out the shifts. Me and Buck were ready to start down the street on our first circuit when someone gave a frightened curse.

I looked up. I couldn't see it at first, but in a moment it grew clearer. An orange glow had begun to spread across the plain, growing broader and more intense as it surged in our direction like an incoming tide.

The wave crashed upon the town, a stampede of cattle, all ablaze in the dark. It was not only that their backs were on fire, as I had seen men do to livestock to terrorize a village or a line of troops, but they were afire from nose to tail complete, a conflagration thundering toward us. They left a trail of molten tallow that dripped from their flanks as it was rendered from their flesh. Their eyes had boiled away, and I could see charred bone poking through split hide.

"I cain't see how they're still running," Buck said, awestruck.

The cattle crashed through town blindly, running through the alleys, dripping flame upon the boardwalks. I watched as one crashed into the lobby of White's Hotel, and that orange glow flickered through the first floor of the building. Another scrambled madly through the wide front window of Lopez's general store. They made no sound themselves, their lungs and vocal cords no doubt cooked away already. They reached the church, some barreling up the steps and down the aisle toward the pulpit where Dell stood in shock. He was still hollering hellfire and damnation when they smashed through the pulpit and one took him on his horns and carried him flailing back into the presbytery. I could hear the screams now from all over, and people running in the street now ablaze themselves.

There, astride a great long-horned bull that must have gone three thousand pounds in life, came the hanged man, the noose around his neck unaffected by the fire that engulfed him and his steed. There was the sound of a shotgun blast behind me and I looked back to see one of the boys collapse. The shotgun he'd held to his own chin trailed smoke.

This whole town is gonna burn.

Well. Maybe burned is what we all got coming.

The Skinhead
and the Cavalier
Kevin Lauderdale

THIS LITTLE TOWN WAS SO hokey that they didn't
even know Gunner was a skinhead. They just thought he
was bald.

Gunner sighed. It was looking less and less like he'd be
able to pull off a robbery of any worth around here.
There just wasn't anything to steal.

Gunner lay back on the park bench. It was late
afternoon, and he was alone. The park hadn't been kept-
up all that well. Some bushes were overgrown, and the
grass needed a trim. But the lawn itself was big: about one
square city block. It was dotted with half a dozen black,
wrought-iron benches, and there was a huge bronze
statue of a man on a horse in the park's center. Even
from where he was laying, Gunner could see the name
carved deep in the statue's granite pedestal: Col.
Forthright Avery. The dates were from the Civil War, and
the horse's right front hoof was raised. That meant the

colonel had been wounded in action. If both front legs had been raised, that would have meant he died in battle. Four hooves on the ground meant he had died outside of battle. Maybe of gout or consumption, or whatever it was that killed people back then. Or maybe just of old age.

Gunner wondered how many people knew that about statues. Not many anymore. Not that it mattered. That business with statues and paintings—*"See how the three figures form a triangle, and the eye is drawn to the apex." Yeah. Whatever*—was all so worthless. He only knew it because it had been foisted on him before his *real* education had begun. Before he had learned about all the conspiracies and how foreigners were keeping America down.

And how he should do his part stop it.

It was getting warm. As Gunner took off his battered, green fatigue jacket, he turned and could just make out the town's sign. It was metal, with white letters on a black field. The upper right corner of the sign was beaten up and folded, dog-eared. He wondered what kind of metal that was. You could probably bend tin pretty easily, but not steel.

Welcome to
Collier, North Carolina
Population 359

359! That meant it was smaller than Lynchburg, Tennessee, where they made Jack Daniels. Gunner had never been to Tennessee, but he'd seen more than his share of bottles of Jack in his twenty-two years. And every single bottle had Lynchburg's population right there on the label: 361.

Too bad Collier didn't have any. How could a place be "plum out"? Not just of Jack, but of everything strong.

Of course, even if there had been a state liquor store in Collier, he didn't have the money for Jack (not even a fifth), but he'd hoped to pick up a little something, even just a Bud, while casing that joint. Gunner laughed. How could a place that dinky *not* be out? The store was called Taylor's Ordinary—an actual general store! *God, how friggin' Tom Sawyer.* Not a Food Lion or even a Piggly Wiggly, but a general store. And one without anything worth stealing. The lady behind the counter had smiled and suggested he might like one of their nice new pairs of jeans, though. "Looks like you've grown a might, young man." Stupid bitch. She'd obviously never seen Levis properly rolled up to show off just the right amount of Doc Martens.

In the end, he hadn't bought anything.

Gunner looked back down Collier's main drag—he wasn't even going to check; it *had* to be named Main Street—then up the other way. Nobody around. The only people he'd seen since he'd wandered into town that morning had been a couple of shop owners and about as many customers. They had looked at him with the usual small town ah-a-stranger glance, but nothing more. They obviously didn't recognize a real patriot when they saw one.

At least they were all white.

Even this late, the sun was really beating down on Gunner's skull. Most people didn't even know why skinheads shaved their heads: because they were so proud of their white skin that they wanted to show as much of it as possible. At that moment, though, Gunner wished he had a hat.

Smitty had told him that about their heads months ago when Gunner had first joined up. It only now occurred to him that Smitty had a whole bunch of tattoos. Didn't tattoos cover up skin? In fact—

Gunner froze. What was that smell? It was sweet and tangy... He closed his eyes and slowly turned his head, all the better to zero in on it without any distractions. It was a ripe smell, an earthy and juicy smell.

Was that peach pie? His Gran used to make peach pie back when he was a kid. Back when his name was Geoffrey. Before.

The smell was coming from his left. He stood up and started making his way along the north side of the park. He knew it was the north side because moss was growing on the trees facing him. More useless knowledge.

The house was a two-story Colonial just across the street. A breeze must have carried the smell to him. *So that really happens*, thought Gunner. *How about that*. It was a brick house that had been painted white. It had a red front door. The kitchen was on his left.

Was that a pie actually cooling on an open window sill? He'd seen that in Bugs Bunny cartoons, but not real life. This was the twenty-first century. Didn't these people have fans in their kitchens? Or refrigerators, for God's sake!

No, wait. You couldn't put a something hot from the oven right into a fridge. Trapped in that space, the heat would radiate out and—

Gunner shook his head to clear it. His brain was just stuffed full of useless junk like that.

Well, he sure as hell hadn't come to Collier just to steal a pie! That wouldn't get him anywhere.

The whole idea was to score some cash so he could get a bus ticket up north to a big city and find some folks in the Skin Nation. Two days of walking had only got him as far as this hokey place. If he wanted to get any further—on to Rockingham, or even Laurinburg—he was going to have to score something more substantial than friggin' flour and fruit.

He had a gun, and he had bullets, but no car, so he couldn't make any sort of a getaway. There was no point in knocking over some store or trying to steal anything heavy. It was going to have to be something that he could take without anybody noticing for a while. Something small and valuable that he could carry off and pawn.

Still, that pie smelled awfully good. And he hadn't had anything to eat all day.

Gunner looked through the window into the kitchen. The floor was yellow linoleum flecked with gold, and there was one of those old fashioned, white, waist-high freezers that was about as big as a businessman's desk. Gunner imagined you could stick a whole deer in it. Yeah, roadkill cuisine—that was about the speed here in Collier. There was a refrigerator after all: avocado green. What was this, his Gran's kitchen? And that stove—

Something shiny caught his eyes.

The door to the living room was open, and there was something on the wall closest to the kitchen. It was round, and at first Gunner thought it was a clock, since it was about as big as dinner plate. He stared. Soon he could make out that it wasn't a shiny *thing*, but dozens of things that were shiny parts of the whole. Behind him, a breeze rustled a tree branch, throwing, for just a moment, a shadow on the interior of the house. In that glareless second, he saw that they were coins.

Coins! Perfect! Not for spending themselves, of course. In a frame, on display, they were probably from the Civil War or Medieval England or something. Great. Anybody might have a collection of old coins to sell; they wouldn't arouse suspicion. They didn't have serial numbers. They were exactly the sort of things that would fetch something in a pawnshop.

Of course, Collier didn't have one of those either. He hadn't even seen a bank or a McDonald's. They did have two churches though. Not that he'd be stupid enough to try to pawn something stolen in a small town to a pawnshop in the same small town. Oh, that'd be good. *Hey, I gave this to Mary Alice just last Christmas—freeze right there, young man!* No, he—Wait! A coin shop! A real coin collector place. Sure, any town of a reasonable size would have one of those. He could get some *real* money there: bus fare and some walking-around money. Hell, he could even break up the set: sell half in one town, half in another. If anyone came looking for them, they'd be looking for two dozen or so, not one.

Should he climb in now? Just hop up and—

With a series of loud creaks, the hem of a blue gingham dress appeared. Someone descended the stairs to the living room. Gunner turned and walked away rapidly.

He'd come back in a few hours at night. He'd just lay low in the thickest part of the park's bushes and come back after the lightning bugs had all gone dark.

This was the sort of place where they left their windows and doors open at night to catch the cool breezes. And if they did close them, they didn't lock them.

The window was still open.

The pie was gone.

Gunner slipped both hands under the window pane and slid it up a little more—

"*BARK!*"

What the—?

"BARKBARKBARKBARK!"

A dog! The barking was a fast, savage, angry sound. He could almost hear it in English: "My house! My, my, my house!"

The lights came on upstairs.

Gunner fled.

He was really hungry now. He wished he'd stolen the pie when he'd had the chance.

"Would you like another piece of pie?"

"Yes, ma'am, it's delicious," said Gunner.

And it *was* delicious. He didn't have to lie about that. The old lady—Mrs. Dilmore—had made a pie that tasted shockingly like his Gran's. It wasn't just the flavors of cinnamon and nutmeg—and tapioca. He *knew* there was tapioca in there somewhere. That made all the difference in the world. It was texture too; each peach still had some firmness to it. If he closed his eyes, he could almost hear his Gran whistling in the kitchen as she made him lunch, slicing those hard-boiled eggs with that wire cutter and pouring milk into a tall, green, plastic glass with sparkles on it that made it look like a Christmas tree ornament. . .

Gunner shook his head, trying to clear out the memories. All of that was from Before.

It had been laughably easy to con his way into Mrs. Dilmore's place. "Pardon me, ma'am... just passing through... could you direct me to... yes, it is a warm one... some lemonade? Oh, ma'am, I couldn't impose... you insist? Some *fresh* peach pie?"

Maybe it was that Ol' Fabled Southern Hospitality. Or maybe she was lonely. She lived alone, and in these tiny towns if your relatives moved away, you only saw them once a year—if that. Also, she looked really old. Any friends she had had were probably long dead. Or maybe the one was born of the other. When you lived in a small town, you probably got really tired of seeing the same 358 people over and over. *Of course* you were happy to see a stranger. *Of course* you welcomed him in. Like back when people used to fight wars over things like cinnamon. They were desperate for something to literally add spice to their lives. Anything to break up the monotony.

Gunner just sat back on the living room couch and enjoyed another bite.

From behind the couch came a trotting, clicking sound.

"Ahh," said Mrs. Dilmore. "There's my Dixie."

The clicking—toenails on the hardwood floor, it turned out—stopped, and a blur jumped onto the old lady's lap.

That was the guard dog?! It was a little spaniel! Only about as big as a large cat.

"You silly girl," said Mrs. Dilmore to the dog, scratching the bridge of its nose. The dog's mouth was half-open, panting. "Where were you? Asleep in the W.C., most likely." She turned to Gunner. "Dixie Belle loves to nap on cool, tile floors—the W.C., the kitchen…"

"A Cavalier King Charles spaniel," muttered Gunner. Yep, he knew some worthless stuff about King Charles II: "James and Charles, and Charles and James, those are the names." He'd learned that "useful" way to memorize that the Kings of England before and after Oliver Cromwell went James I, Charles I, Charles II, and James II. Kings of England! When was he ever going to need to know that? He'd also learned which dogs were their favorites. More of his fake education. And Dixie looked just like those dogs you saw in Old Master paintings… if you were the sort of person who went to museums. Gunner wasn't—anymore.

Dixie's fur was white with large patches of brown. Her feathery, floppy ears were brown; and brown circled her eyes, but left her muzzle white, making her look like she was wearing a robber's mask. She had a brown spot about the size of a thumb-print on the top of her head.

In the minutes he'd been in the living room, Gunner had been discretely studying the coin display out of the corner of an eye. There were about two dozen coins, arranged in concentric circles, most silver, some a chocolaty copper. Many were odd sizes: dark discs smaller than dimes, and thick, silver-blue circles larger than even silver dollars. All of his attention had been centered on the coins... and the pie. Only now that the dog was there did the rest of the living room seem to appear from nowhere. It was like he had been on a stage with spotlights on just himself, the old lady, and the coins on the wall. Now, the rest of the stage was finally illuminated.

Gunner saw that Mrs. Dilmore collected all manner of Cavalier things. There were bookshelves full of the crap: little china Cavaliers sitting posed at attention, big ones that looked like they were Cavalier cookie jars... There was a print of a painting of one by some famous French artist. There was even a *needlepoint* of one above the fireplace mantle! They were everywhere. *Geeze, lady, get a life!*

"You like my Cavaliers," said Mrs. Dilmore. It was a statement, not a question. "They're just so cute." She slowly stroked the dog's neck. "But not as cute as you, Dixie Belle."

Dixie rubbed her head against the old lady's hand and wagged her tail. The fur on her tail spread out like a fan.

Friggin' dog.

A teapot whistled from the kitchen. "Oh, off I go," said Mrs. Dilmore. She slid Dixie from her lap onto the couch then left, flower-print house dress flapping behind her.

The dog watched her mistress leave, then turned and stared at Gunner.

Oh, yeah, right, thought Gunner. *Like you even saw me last night. Right.*

Dixie growled at Gunner with a low rumble and gave him a terrible squinting look.

Mrs. Dilmore came back in, and the dog immediately stopped.

Mrs. Dilmore set her tea pot down on a trivet featuring a Cavalier's face, then sat herself down. Dixie climbed back into the old lady's lap. The dog turned to Gunner and gave him that same insipid, mouth-half-open panting look.

Mrs. Dilmore laughed. "Some people say dogs can't laugh, but all they have to do is take one look at Dixie here to know they can." She scratched the dog under the chin. "Look at that expression, that mouth. That's a laugh, like they're in on some great, cosmic joke."

Cosmic joke! What a cliché!

She scratched Dixie under her chin some more then bent down a bit and kissed the brown thumbprint spot on the dog's head. "It's called a 'Blenheim spot'—the mark of a true Cavalier. But I call it a 'kissing spot.'"

Gunner nodded. *Ewww.* He wouldn't kiss a dog any sooner than he'd kiss a rat. Some of the stuff he'd seen dogs eat… and they were always licking their behinds. He wouldn't put his mouth anywhere near a dog's head.

Friggin' dog.

Later, three-quarters of the pie gone, Mrs. Dilmore led him out a side door that led to the sleeping porch screened off against mosquitoes. The lock on it was an insubstantial one like you would find on any cheap screen door. It was just a little bump of metal filling a tiny hole. Gunner figured one quick yank would pop it open.

Around midnight, it popped open even more quietly than Gunner had hoped.

In seconds, he was back in the living room.

It was dark, which was something he hadn't thought about nor planned for. But he had spent a good forty-five minutes in the living room just a few hours before. He was sure he knew where things were. And his eyes were adjusting more and more with each second.

As he inched towards the couch, he could hear a low, rumbling sound.

Snoring.

Oh, great, was the old lady sleeping down here tonight? He edged closer. No. It was the stupid dog.

A snoring dog?! What the hell?! And this wasn't a tiled floor. What was she doing, waiting for him?

"Looks like," Gunner whispered, "you've fallen asleep on the job, you little bitch." He smiled. *Bitch.* Ha! That was a good one.

He stepped closer to the coins, and the old floor creaked. He snapped his head back to the dog. The dog's paws fluttered, but her snoring continued.

Gunner couldn't take the chance of the dog waking up and going all psycho on him.

He fingered the Beretta in his jacket pocket.

He could use one of those throw pillows as a silencer. If he could just find one without a lousy dog on it.

Ah, there was one: a simple blue pillow, about as big as dictionary but soft. Probably made by hand by the old lady and stuffed with chicken feathers or something.

He raised his gun against the pillow, aimed, and shot.

There was a muffled CRACK! and Dixie's legs jerked for just a second. Right in the head. Right through the "kissing spot." There was blood and a mess. He didn't like leaving anything that might draw attention, but the plans had changed. He was tired of this tiny town and tired of sleeping in the park. He was getting out *tonight*.

There. That was that little problem solved. He tossed the pillow back on a chair and turned around to—

Growl.

Gunner froze. What the hell was that? He looked back over his shoulder. Yep, the dog was still there. Still dead. He sighed a little with relief. He had thought some weird, Stephen King thing was going on.

Growwwwl!

He spun around, gun at the ready to waste… what, some other dog that had wandered in? Or did the old lady actually have more than one?

Gunner was not prepared for what he saw.

Cavaliers.

Dozens of them stood facing him. They stood on the couch and the on the floor, an army of brown and white, their ears cocked back and their teeth bared as they growled and advanced.

Their teeth! Had Dixie had such sharp, glistening teeth?

The closest one barked and lunged at Gunner. He fired his gun, but he missed, or else it somehow had no effect, because the dog landed on his throat. He tried to pry it off, but it hung with a tenacity he hadn't counted on. He pulled again, and felt the agony of the teeth ripping at his muscles. The thing weighed about twenty pounds and all of that was concentrated on his throat. Then another dog tore at one leg, and another at his other leg. Two more jumped at his stomach, their combined weight knocking him to the floor.

Then they were all upon him. They carved through his clothes and into his body everywhere. He felt the shock of their teeth scraping against his own bones. He tried to pull them off him, but they were on his arms now as well. And there were too many of them.

He shook his head violently, trying to get them off his face, but it was no use. His last thought before he plunged into the darkness was to wonder if someone else had already robbed the place. From where he lay, he couldn't see if the coins were still there, but the bookshelves were empty.

Fallen Angels
Jessica West

Virgil Dunn, The Rusty Spur, 1865

SHE TURNED HEADS just the way you'd expect a woman with fine curves and long hair might when she sashayed into a saloon at midnight. Over in the corner, Turner quit hammerin' the keys long enough to find out why he was suddenly the only one making a racket. Damn shame, too. The room was just getting nice and warmed up. Even Hazel, miss high and mighty herself, had come down from her tower–which was nothing but a loft in the rafters above the second-floor bedrooms–to join the singing. And she only ever came out for the soldiers. But when she walked in, everyone–and I do mean everyone–stopped for a good, long gander.

I waited 'til she got closer to the counter to ask her, "What can I do ya for?" Wasn't necessarily trying to be dirty. It's just the way I talk to folks who show up in my bar. It's a running joke. Never gets old. She sure didn't seem to think so. She gave me one of those sly little smiles a woman'll give you. You know the one. Makes you a little weak in the knees and a lot weak in the head.

"I'm more interested in what I can do her for." She waved a hand in the general direction of upstairs, her white glove shining like a beacon in the harsh lights of the smoke-filled room.

Now, I'm no blushing bride, but I damn near fainted like one. "Come again?"

When she turned those crystal blue eyes on me, I forgot my name for a second. I'd have handed over damn near anything she wanted, and not just because she was so mesmerizing. There was something else I was feeling, something that kept the firmness in my pants from becoming all-out painful. Fear. Can't rightly say why, but I was more than a little scared of her now that I think of it.

You ever look real close at a shard of broken glass? It's pretty in its own way, in a way that nothing else is. It'll fuck your day right up if you're not careful, but it's real pretty. She seemed like that: a shard of broken glass.

When she asked again…well, like I said, with her eyes focused directly on me like they were, I'd have given her anything she wanted.

"I'd like a room for the night and the company of its occupant. Preferably the room at the top."

Hazel was gonna kill me, but I could no more have told her no than I could have chopped off my own pecker. "Need some help with your bags?"

"No, thank you." She lifted a small bag in front of her. I couldn't tell you what it was made of, but that was the fanciest damn bag I'd ever seen. "I've only got the one. I can manage."

Instead of showing her up to the room, I followed her up the stairs. Hazel was fuming all the while, but she never said a word. She might have acted like she owned the place, but she knew good and well whose roof was over her head. The matter was settled and if she didn't like it, she knew where the door was.

That woman walked into Hazel's room like she owned it, and Hazel followed her. Slammed the damn door before I could say goodnight. Can't say I blame her.

I never saw the woman again after that, and the next time I saw Hazel, she was dead.

Virginia Claiborne, The White Dove Society, 1869

My sister was a good, morally sound woman. Only a little bit rebellious. But when those two daughters of sin came to town, everyone changed.

Irving Harmon helped build half the buildings in this town with his own bare hands. Grace, that was his wife, she showed up early to church every Sunday morning with food for the whole congregation. Never you mind there weren't many of us. Feeding a dozen or more people is quite the chore. But she always had plenty of freshly made biscuits and the most delicious jams you ever tasted. But those women went to work on her first. I should have taken Isabel and run when I saw what they did to Grace. But I never thought things would go as far as they did.

Come out onto the porch. I want to show you something.

Look across the road there, at the saloon. Up, in the window. See her? Can't help but see her, with her hands and face pressed up against the glass like that. God knows who's pounding away at her right now, in full view of the whole damn town. If old Henry tells it true, that's how Grace likes it. Makes me sick. Her poor husband's probably rolling in his grave. Not that she'd care. She's probably the one who done him in. She got caught up with those two women. Started acting real strange. We knew there was a problem when she stopped coming to church, but what could we do?

I went out to her house early one Sunday morning, hoping to coax her back to church. She hadn't been in a few weeks. I'll never get that horrific image out of my mind. They were in the kitchen, Grace and Irving. Him leaning back against the table and her on her knees in front of him. I'd rather not say just what she was doing, but his britches were on the floor and I couldn't see his manhood for her head in the way. So you can just about imagine. And the sounds! Goodness, you'd think she was gobbling up pie the way she was... *Ugh*. She was *sucking* on that thing. Can you imagine?

I high-tailed it out of there right quick fast and in a hurry. Never looked back. Unfortunately, that scene was only the first of many that would play out all over town. I started seeing Grace everywhere, and not in a way a lady should be seen. At the grocer's, I could hear Peter panting in the back room. Naturally, I thought he was moving something heavy, maybe those sacks of flour. Come to find out she was riding him like a horse. In broad daylight! And right there in the stock room of his store.

Worse, I caught her and Pastor Leonard in his room above the church. I was only going up there because he wasn't in his office. I had a habit of meeting up with him...for spiritual talks, you know...every Sunday after church. But that day, he wasn't there. So I climbed the stairs and I could hear Grace. The way she was carrying on, I figured he'd put the fear of God into her for sure. I thought maybe he had straightened her out. But when I peeked through the keyhole, I saw her sitting on his face, hips rocking back and forth, his hands on her bottom. At first I thought he was trying to get her off of him. But he was gripping her so hard, his fingertips sank into her flesh like he had her exactly where he wanted her. His manhood was straight as a rod, and that's when I knew he was corrupted.

All because Grace had taken them in, those two harlots. No telling what they did to that poor woman and Irving. All we know is what we were left with: Grace whoring all over town and Isabel gone.

I should have taken Isabel and run.

Sheriff Samuel Hobbs, Last Crossing, 1973

Those three girls have been giving me hell for the better part of a year. I had an easier time tracking down the Ebony Skull gang, and those boys were slicker than a rattlesnake in a mudhole. Now don't get me wrong, women giving hell ain't nothing new. Hell, I have a great deal of respect for women like Belle at the saloon. Say what you will about painted ladies, but she's got one helluva head for business. But she's a good woman. A good person. But those three girls? That's a whole other kind of hell.

Anybody tell you what they did up at the Dyer place? No? Well, I reckon that's no surprise. Folks don't like to talk *about that*, and they generally like to talk. It's just as well you hear the story from me. I may not know all of it, but I know more than I was willing to let on. Some things are better left untold. Some things, I wish even I didn't know.

Chester and Lola Dyer were good people. No kids, and even though Lola was tore up about that I can't help but think now it was a blessing. Or maybe the lack of children was what led those three to the Dyers in the first place. I guess we'll never know.

They rode into town hours before a helluva storm was due to hit, begging for a place to spend the night. Chester happened to be at the saloon when they waltzed in.

Don't get me wrong, Chester was a good man and a good husband. He loved Lola. But the longer she went without catchin', the colder she was to him. Hell, before those girls showed up, Lola was downright mean. It wasn't her fault, not really. She just wanted a baby so bad. For about three weeks, she'd lain with any man who'd have her. She'd go home to Chester and tell him if he'd given her a baby, she wouldn't have to be out whoring. He once told me he understood why she did it. He couldn't give her what she needed. But once she crossed that line, she couldn't give him what he needed either. Chester never would raise his hand or his voice to her; he'd just go off to the saloon to get what he couldn't get at home. That's what done him in.

As luck would have it, Chester had come to the saloon late that night. Probably because Lola had been out late with Pete, but I don't reckon that part of the story bears repeatin' now. All the girls were occupied, so he had to wait his turn. Turner Copeland took pity on him. He stopped playing long enough to sit with him at the bar. When those three walked in, the whole room got real quiet. Like time stopped.

The one in the middle slowly looked around the room, taking her time with each face, meeting every pair of eyes with her icy blue ones. When she locked that gaze on me, I could have died right there. I'm not sure how it happened, but we ended up riding out of town together—me, Chester, Turner and those three girls—headed out to Chester's place. I didn't offer the use of my place on account of it being so small. And Turner's place...well, he didn't offer and we didn't think to ask. So, Chester's it was.

Lola was sittin' in the kitchen, eyes red and face wet. She knew where he'd been. Everything that passed between them was out in the open. Didn't hurt either one of them any less, but there were no secrets between them.

Chester told Lola, "Go on over to Harriet's tonight. Or stay."

For about a minute solid, it looked like she'd put up some kind of fight. But that one with the icy eyes locked gazes with her and she just shut the door behind us. "Weather's getting to rough to ride out now. Might as well stay."

I won't repeat the things that happened that night, but I woke up sometime after the worst of the storm had passed and high-tailed it out of there like my hair was on fire and my ass was catchin'. Never saw Turner again, but Chester's remains were there when I went back the next day. Him and Lola were laid up in the bed like they were sleeping. I might have believed it, wouldn't have even gone inside to check if not for all the blood.

Those women left bodies and blood wherever they went. Made it easy to track them, but I always found cold corpses or grisly stories by the time I made it to wherever they landed. The women's heads were always missing. The only reason I knew it was Lola's body in the bed is because...well, hell, just about every man in town had enjoyed a visit. Any one of us could have told you it was her.

And we never did find any of the heads. Tell you the truth, I'm almost glad I was never able to catch up to them. But I owe it to Chester and Lola to try. If you find them, you put 'em down quick.

I picked up where Sheriff Hobbs left off in 1973. I tracked the three fallen angels to Arizona, to the doorstep—such as it was—of Catherine Cartwright and her odd bunch. She was shacked up in the woods with a cowboy, I forget his name, and a pair of Navahos—a young woman and a man whose age I couldn't guess. They asked what kind of bullets I kept in my gun.

"You'll need silver," Cat said. "But not for them."

And the West only got weirder from there.

The Lost Tapes:
Future Told
Daniel Arthur Smith

"RECORDING BEGINS WITH today's date, November 30th, 2019. My name is Agent Melissa Muldoon. Present with me is Agent Lawrence Meyer. Commencing interview of one Professor Charles Rampart. Dr. Rampart is a professor of Anthropology at the university and...is this right? You're a psychic?"

"Not really. No."

"But you do claim to have the ability to see into the future?"

"Not 'see,' necessarily. I experience events in and out of time. Past, future, present of course."

"You're a medium then?"

"Uh. Okay. I suppose–if you were to put a label on it–clairvoyant maybe?"

"So you believe you're clairvoyant?"

"Sounds better than time traveler."

"Fair enough. I'll make the correction here in the file...and let's go again. Commencing interview of one Professor Charles Rampart. Dr. Rampart claims to have the clairvoyant ability to see into the future. He has come forward with information regarding a homicide and has agreed to this interview willingly. Mr. Rampart, can you please state your name for the record?"

"Yes...It's Charlie Rampart, Charles, Charles Rampart, but you can call me Charlie. All the kids do. Professor Charlie, they say."

"Thank you for meeting with us. When you called, you stated, in your words, 'you had information pertaining to a murder.'"

"Murders. More than one."

"Huh. Again, I'll make a correction in the file. Okay. There. It says that you didn't state to which homicide–homicides–you were referring. Could you please be more specific? For the record."

"These murders, homicides as you call them, haven't occurred yet."

"Excuse me?"

"They haven't happened. Not yet, anyway."

"Is this in reference to a terrorist threat?

"No, not terrorists. A serial killer."

"How did you come by this information?"

"I've seen them. The homicides, I mean."

"Aha. In the future?"

"Yes."

"Dr. Rampart—"

"Charlie. Please."

"Charlie. If you have reason to believe that someone, or any number of individuals, are in danger, we have to act immediately."

"I understand that. That's why I'm here. It seems the killer is murdering psychics and fortune-tellers."

"All of the victims are clairvoyants, like yourself?"

"Yes. And no. I mean they're not like me, or maybe they are. One is an astrologist, another works as a psychic, and the other two call themselves fortunetellers, but I don't know if they can really experience the future or if they're putting on an act."

"But the commonality is that they are at least perceived as clairvoyant."

"Yes. It is."

"And you believe you're being targeted as well."

"I know I am."

"And how do you know this?"

"I told you. I've seen it."

"And how is that?"

"I'll explain it like this. With the assistance of a chemical cocktail, I'm able to reach an advanced meditative state that allows me to experience what you call the future."

"Chemical cocktail?"

"A mix of DMT and psilocybin."

"Oh. I see."

"I know, I know. It sounds cliché—crazy old anthropology teacher going native. But it's an age-old thing. Shamans and mystics have been performing ritualistic meditation since the dawn of man."

"You wouldn't be the first anthropology professor I've met who's gone native."

"Ha, ha. Get your digs in, but even the Dalai Lama performs a similar practice. Have you ever heard of the Kalachakra?"

"I'm familiar with the Dalai Lama, and the Kalachakra. The wheel of time."

"Yeah. That's right. The Wheel of Time. And do you know what it represents?"

"That's the idea that there's no present without the past or future. But isn't it just an awareness practice, a form of meditation?"

"It's more than that. Have you ever heard of the B-theory of time?"

"Sure. I remember a bit from school. All points in time are equal. As humans, we only experience them in passing. Yada, yada."

"Right. We experience time like a movie. The projector rolls and we take in events in a linear fashion, one at a time, one after another. But if you stopped the projector and pulled the film from the reel, you could see all the frames at once. The past, present, and future, all equal before you."

"Okay. But that's your movie."

"That's right. I can only see my future, my past."

"Then how did you witness these yet to be homicides?"

"I didn't see the act. I saw the crime scene."

"You've seen them after the fact?"

"I'm going to. Yes. You ask'll me about them, and I'll give you the names. You hold me here while you check them out. Everybody seems okay, you think

I'm crazy, and then reports of the murders come in the way I'll describe."

"Before you're released?"

"Uhuh."

"You're speaking as if this has already happened."

"To me, to my experience, it has."

"And how will we stop the killer...I mean if the homicides, as you've just stated, are predetermined to happen?"

"We can't stop her. We never could. But we can catch her. In fact, you do."

"When?"

"Why, at my own murder, of course."

"At your murder?"

"Yes. You and Agent Meyer are with me when she attempts to kill me. You catch her in the act. But, unfortunately, too late to save me."

"I see. Can you excuse me for a moment?"

...

"Well, Director Higgins. What do you think? He said he was at the crime scenes. That's practically a confession."

"But he hasn't been there yet?"

"He just admitted he was...or will be."

"Well, we'll contact those people he listed and put them under protection. We'll keep him here on a hold for the next seventy-two hours and restrict his communication."

"You think he's not working alone?"

"He'll have an alibi. If on the remote chance he's right and something does happen, I think you'll take him to the crime scenes as he laid out."

"Why would I do that?"

"To catch the killer, of course. According to him, the killer is going to approach him."

"I guess we'll see."

ABOUT THE AUTHORS

Steve Oden has worked in the publishing industry—mainly newspapers and magazines—for more than 30 years. Although retired, he provides editorial services on a consulting basis, mainly to corporate clients, and writes on assignment. His newspaper columns have appeared regularly in Tennessee and Alabama publications since 1980, winning awards from the Alabama Press Association, University of Tennessee-Tennessee Press Association, Society of Professional Journalists, National Rural Electric Cooperative Association and several wildlife conservation organizations.

K.H. Vaughan a refugee from academia with a Ph.D. in clinical psychology. In his other life he taught, published, and practiced in various settings, with particular interest in decision theory, forensic psychology, psychopathology, and methodology. He lives with his wife and three children in New England. He is an editor emeritus with Dark Discoveries Magazine and Hellnotes.com and writes speculative fiction including horror, science fiction, and fantasy.

His official webpage can be found at www.khvaughan.net, and he is also on Facebook.

Kevin Lauderdale written essays and articles for the *Los Angeles Times*, *The Dictionary of American Biography,* and **McSweeneys.net**. His short fiction has appeared in several of Pocket Books' *Star Trek* anthologies as well as various small press publications. His story "Box 27" was published in the science journal *Nature*. This is his fourth appearance in Canyons of the Damned. He hosts the Old Time Radio podcast, *"Presenting the Transcription Feature,"* and co-hosts *"Temple of Bad,"* the podcast about movies that are so bad, they're practically a religious experience, both on the Chronic Rift network. He is a member of SFWA and HWA.

Jessica West (a.k.a. West1Jess) is currently pursuing a state of self-induced psychosis, also known as writing. In the past, she has worked for Wal-Mart, a lawyer, and a bank. Now if she could just get a couple years experience with the IRS and the NSA, world domination is in the bag.
Jess lives in Acadiana with three daughters still young enough to think she's cool and a husband who knows better but likes her anyway.

For news and updates visit west1jess.com

Daniel Arthur Smith is a USA Today bestselling author. His titles include *Spectral Shift, Hugh Howey Lives, The Cathari Treasure, The Somali Deception*, and a few other novels and short stories. He also curates the phenomenal short fiction series *Tales from the Canyons of the Damned* and *Frontiers of Speculative Fiction*.

He was raised in Michigan and graduated from Western Michigan University where he studied philosophy, with focus on cognitive science, meta-physics, and comparative religion. He began his career as a bartender, barista, poetry house proprietor, teacher, and then became a technologist and futurist for the Fortune 100 across the Americas and Europe.

Daniel has traveled to over 300 cities in 22 countries, residing in Los Angeles, Kalamazoo, Prague, Crete, and now writes in Manhattan where he lives with his wife and young sons.

For news and updates visit danielarthursmith.com